TOOT & PUDDLE

Puddle's

ABC

TOOT & PUDDLE

Puddle's

by

Holly Hobbie

Little, Brown and Company

Boston   New York   London

First Edition

Library of Congress Cataloging-in-Publication Data

Hobbie, Holly.
Toot and Puddle : Puddle's ABC / by Holly Hobbie.
p.   cm.
Summary: Puddle teaches his friend Otto the letters of the alphabet so that Otto can write his name.
ISBN 0-316-36593-9
[1. Pigs — Fiction.   2. Alphabet — Fiction.]   I. Title.   II. Title: Toot and Puddle.
PZ7.H6517Toe   2000
[E] — dc21   99-43277

10 9 8 7 6 5 4 3 2 1

TWP

The paintings for this book were done in watercolors.
The text was set in Optima and the display types are Windsor Light and Poetica.

Printed in Singapore

For readers-to-be

One day Puddle decided to teach Otto how to write his name.

"It starts with O," he said.

"What is O?" asked Otto.

"O is a letter," Puddle told him.

"Oh," said Otto. Then he asked, "Where does the letter O come from?"

Puddle pondered the question. "O comes from the alphabet," he said. "Alphabet?" asked Otto.

"It's not as hard as it sounds," Puddle said.

"The alphabet is all the letters we need in order to write all the words we know," he explained.

"There must be an awful lot of letters," said Otto.

"Not too many," Puddle said. "But you have to learn the letters in order to write words. Like your name: Otto."

"All right," said Otto. "You will have to teach me the letters."

Puddle got busy right away.

Aa

Ant alone
with apple

Bb

Ballerina
blowing
bubbles

Cc

Crocodile
crunching
carrots

Dd

Dirty dog
digging

Ee

Ella
exercising

Ff

Fat firefly
flying fast

Gg

Glowing guppies

Hh
Hippo
hiccuping

I i

Itchy
inchworm

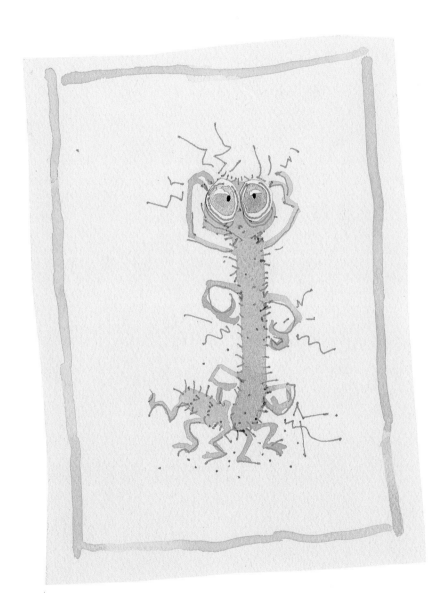

Jj

Jolly jester
juggling

Kk

King-sized
Kiss

Ll

Little lizard
loves
ladybugs

Mm

Miss Mud
in
moonlight

N n

Not another
nightmare!

Oo

Oinkers'
opera

P p

Pretty
in
pink

Qq

Queen
quietly
quilting

Rr

Red
rooster
reading

S s
Someone's
sleeping

Tt

Tip-top
Toot

Uu

Upside down
underwater

Vv

Very
violet

Ww

Woolly bears
waltzing

X x

Excellent
example
of x

Yy

You're
yawning

Zz
Zooming
zucchini

A B C D E F G
H I J K L M N
O P Q R S T U
V W X Y Z

"Practice saying them over and over until you can say them all together," Puddle said.

The next day Otto looked quite proud of himself. "I can say the whole alphabet," he said.

"Now you have to practice *writing* the letters," Puddle said.

So Otto practiced and practiced.

"Now you're ready to write your name," said Puddle.
"It starts with O."
Otto knew what O was. He carefully wrote it with his favorite pencil.

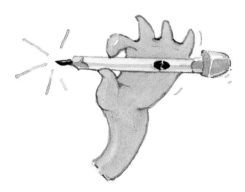

"Then you write T twice," Puddle said.
"Then O again," Toot said.
"That's your name," said Puddle. "You can read it."
"OTTO," Otto said. "I love it!"

OTTO

"I would like to write another name," Otto said.

"Write my name," Toot said. "It starts with T."

Otto knew T. T was easy.

"Then you write O twice," Puddle said.

Otto wrote O twice.

"Then T again," said Toot.

So Otto wrote T again. "TOOT," he said, and his smile was beaming.

Otto then wrote the two words on the same piece of paper.
"They're beautiful," he said.

He looked at the names for quite a while.
At last he said, "OTTO is TOOT spelled inside out."
"You're much smarter than I thought," Toot said.

"You're a genius!" said Puddle. "Let's write another word."

"I would like to write PUDDLE," said Otto.
"Do you know what the first letter is?" Toot asked.
"I think I know," Otto said. And he did know.